Who Took the Cookies from the Cookie Jar?

Read the book, then play the game!

- Form a circle. Give each player an animal name from the story. Choose one player, let's say Skunk, to begin the chant.

- Clap rhythmically, alone or with circle mates, as you say:

Everyone:	Who took the cookies from the cookie jar? (Repeat three times.)
Skunk:	**Raven** took the cookies from the cookie jar!
Raven:	Who, me?
Everyone:	Yes you!
Raven:	Couldn't be!
Everyone:	Then who?
Raven:	**Snake** took the cookies from the cookie jar!
Snake:	Who, me?
Everyone:	Yes you!
Snake:	Couldn't be!
Everyone:	Then who?
Etc.	

- Keep going until all players have had a chance to be "blamed" and then to blame another player.

- To vary the game you may want to give each player a number, a color name, or a letter name. Or you might just let players use their own names!

- The real challenge of the game is to listen for your turn and respond without missing a beat.

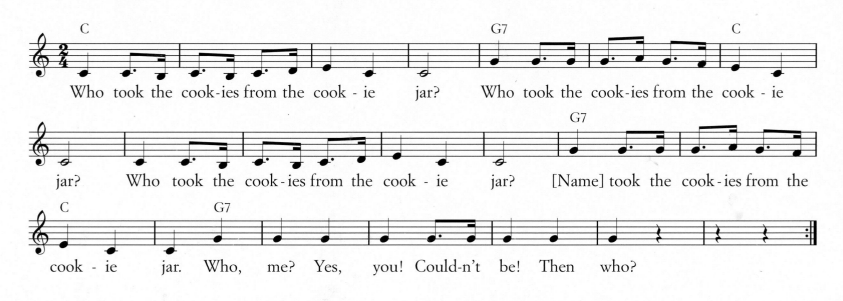

Who took the cook-ies from the cook-ie jar? Who took the cook-ies from the cook-ie

jar? Who took the cook-ies from the cook-ie jar? [Name] took the cook-ies from the

cook-ie jar. Who, me? Yes, you! Could-n't be! Then who?

In memory of the stoops of Park Slope, 1953.
And for my mom, who always gave me
the fifteen cents for a coconut pop.
—B. L.

To Jerry, Betsy, and their cookie-eating pals
Schatzie, Pudsy, Dijon, Ditto, Daisy,
Henry, Traudel, and Molly.
—P. S.

For Judy Taylor,
who always brings the cookies.
—A.W.

Text copyright © 2000 by Bonnie Lass and Philemon Sturges
Illustrations copyright © 2000 by Ashley Wolff

First Edition

Library of Congress Cataloging-in-Publication Data

Lass, Bonnie.
    Who took the cookies from the cookie jar? / by Bonnie Lass and Philemon Sturges ;
    illustrated by Ashley Wolff. — 1st ed.
        p.   cm.
    Summary: A skunk tries to find out which of his animal friends stole the cookies.
    ISBN 0-316-82016-4
    [1. Animals—Fiction. 2. Cookies—Fiction. 3. Food habits—Fiction. 4. Stories in rhyme.]
I. Sturges, Philemon. II. Wolff, Ashley, ill. III. Title.
PZ8.3.L339Wh   2000
[E]—dc21   99-16877

10 9 8 7 6 5 4 3 2 1

TWP

Printed in Singapore

The illustrations for this book were done in watercolor and pen on Arches cover paper.
The text is Simoncini Garamond, and the display type is Jimbo.

by
Bonnie Lass &
Philemon Sturges

Illustrated by
Ashley Wolff

WHO
Took the
COOKIES
from the
COOKIE JAR?

Megan Tingley Books

Little, Brown and Company
Boston New York London

Who took the cookies from the cookie jar?
Who took the cookies from the cookie jar?
Who took the cookies from the cookie jar?

Who took the cookies
From the cookie jar?
The jar was full!
Where did they go?

Mmm ... Oh! ...
Now I know ...

Mouse took the cookies
From the cookie jar!

Who, me?
Couldn't be!
Please don't tease,
I eat cheese.

Then who took the cookies?
The jar was full!
Where did they go?

Mmm ... Oh! ...
Now I know ...

Raven took the cookies
From the cookie jar!

Who, me?
Couldn't be!
Don't squirm,
Eat a worm!

Then who took the cookies?
The jar was full!
Where did they go?

Mmm ... Oh! ...
Now I know ...

Squirrel took the cookies
From the cookie jar!

Who, me?
Couldn't be!
I munch
Nuts for lunch.

Then who took the cookies?
The jar was full!
Where did they go?

Mmm ... Oh! ...
Now I know ...

Rabbit took the cookies
From the cookie jar!

Who, me?
Couldn't be!
Must hop,
Never stop.

Then who took the cookies.
The jar was full!
Where did they go?

Mmm... Oh!...
Now I know...

Turtle took the cookies
From the cookie jar!

Who, me?
Couldn't be!
As you know,
I'm much too slow.

Then who took the cookies?
The jar was full!
Where did they go?

Mmm ... Oh! ...
Now I know ...

Raccoon took the cookies
From the cookie jar!

Who, me?
Couldn't be!
That's crazy,
I'm too lazy.

Then who took the cookies?
The jar was full!
Where did they go?

Mmm ... Oh! ...
Now I know ...

Snake took the cookies
From the cookie jar!

Who, me?
Couldn't be!
I'm stuffed, can hardly speak,
I ate an antelope last week.

Then who took the cookies?
The jar was full!
Where did they go?

Mmm … Oh! …
Now I know …

Beaver took the cookies
From the cookie jar!

Who, me?
Couldn't be!
My favorite snack
Is sticks in a stack.

Then who took the cookies?
The jar was full!
Where did they go?

Mmm... Oh!...
Now I know...

Frog took the cookies
From the cookie jar!

Who, me?
Couldn't be!
Surprise, surprise,
I like gnats and dragonflies!

Then who took the cookies?
The jar was full!
Where did they go?

Mmm... Oh!...
Now I know...

Ants took the cookies
From the cookie jar!

You're right,
It's true.
But there's enough for all of you!

We left a trail to show the way.
So eat your cookies, then let's play!